Lion cub
and the
evil one

4

Lion cub and the evil one
A LION CUB'S ADVENTURES SEASON 1 EPISODE 4:

iUniverse books may be ordered through booksellers or by contacting:

iUniverse
1663 Liberty Drive
Bloomington, IN 47403
www.iuniverse.com
844–349–9409

ISBN: 978-1-6632-1544-4 (sc)
ISBN: 978-1-6632-1545-1 (e)

Library of Congress Control Number: 2020925761

Print information available on the last page.

iUniverse rev. date: 12/29/2020

table of contents

giraffe gorilla elephant and deer share their ideas...

I suggest that we use kangaroo's stick

I suggest that we all attack him at once

I suggest that we banish him from the Jungle

um...can you excuse me and beaver?...we need to think of ideas by ourselves...

go ahead otter and beaver

Panther scratches Lion cubs belly, then gets off him..
you scratched my belly Panther... I'm gonna go fetch my friends..and they'll deal with you!
then run
Pff... you can't escape me that easy...
all right..I will!

chapter 5. a sad scene

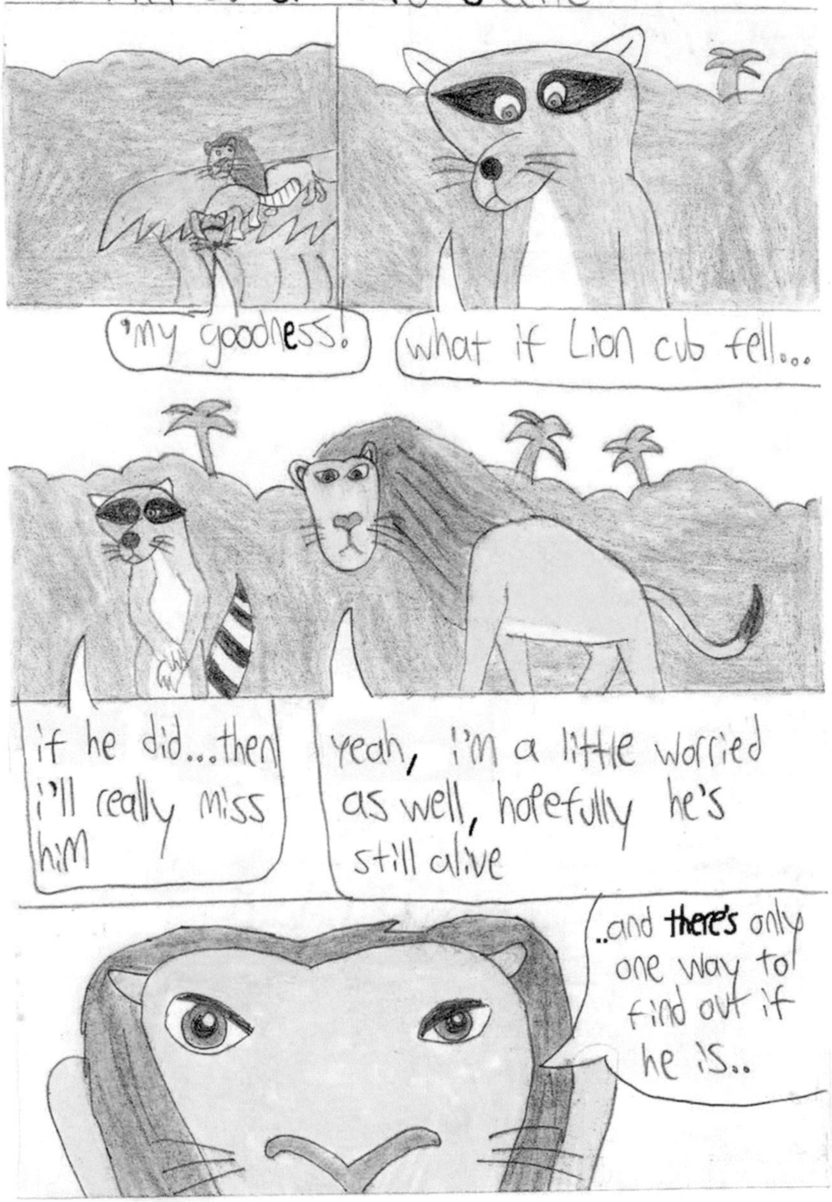

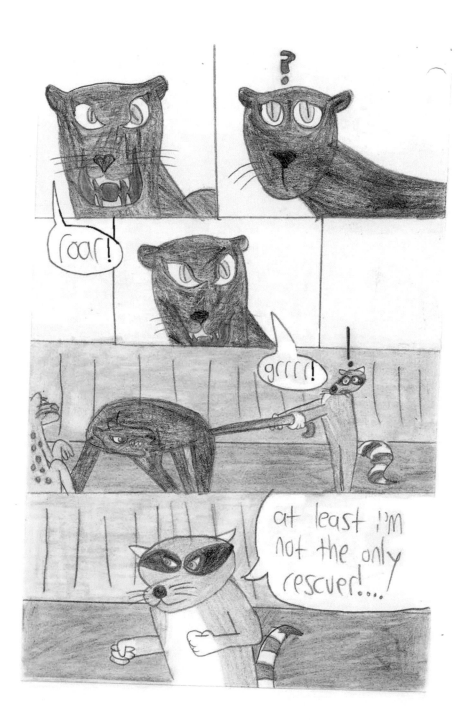

chapter 8. another happy ending

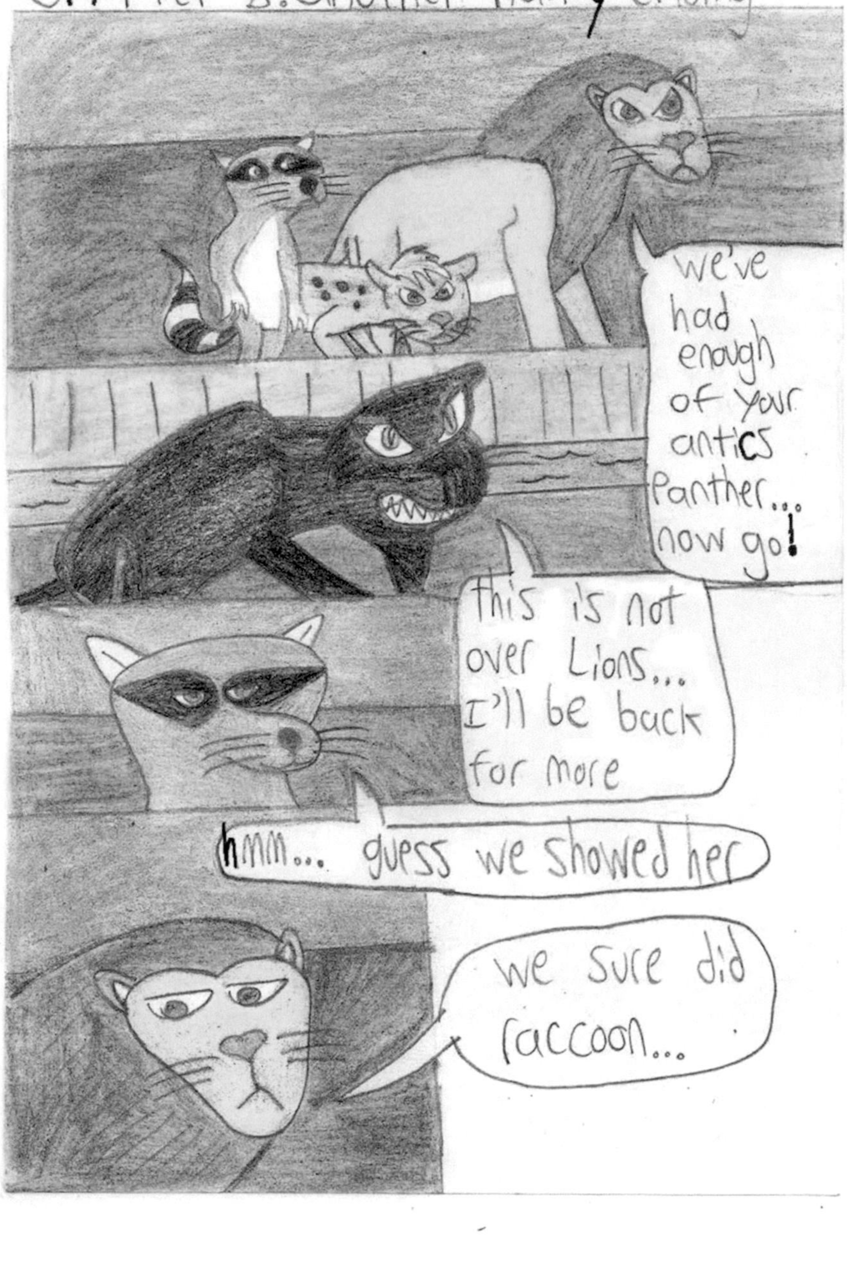

Printed in the United States
By Bookmasters